MURMEL, MURMEL, MURMEL

MURMEL, MURMEL, MURMEL

Story
Robert Munsch

Art
Michael Martchenko

Annick Press Ltd.
Toronto • New York • Vancouver

Twentieth printing, January 2000

Annick Press Ltd.

We acknowledge the support of the Canada Council for the Arts, the Ontario
Arts Council, and the Government of Canada through the Book Publishing Industry
Development Program (BPIDP) for our publishing activities.

Canadian Cataloguing in Publication Data
  Munsch, Robert N., 1945-
    Murmel, murmel, murmel

  (Munsch for kids)
  ISBN 0-920236-29-4 (bound) ISBN 0-920236-31-6 (pbk.)

  I. Martchenko, Michael. II. Title. III. Series:
  Munsch, Robert N., 1945- . Munsch for kids.

  Ps8576.U58M87   jC813'.54   C82-094731-8
  PZ7.M86Mu

Distributed in Canada by:
Firefly Books Ltd.
3680 Victoria Park Avenue
Willowdale, ON
M2H 3K1

Published in the U.S.A. by Annick Press (U.S.) Ltd.
Distributed in the U.S.A. by:
Firefly Books (U.S.) Inc.
P.O. Box 1338
Ellicott Station
Buffalo, NY 14205

Printed and bound in Canada by
Friesens, Altona, Manitoba.

To Andrew, Julie, Robin and Andrea

When Robin went out into her back yard, there was a large hole right in the middle of her sandbox. She knelt down beside it and yelled, "ANYBODY DOWN THERE?"

From way down the hole something said, "Murmel, murmel, murmel."

"Hmmm," said Robin, "very strange." So she yelled, even louder, "ANYBODY DOWN THERE?"

"Murmel, murmel, murmel," said the hole. Robin reached down the hole as far as she could and gave an enormous yank. Out popped a baby.

"Murmel, murmel, murmel," said the baby.

"Murmel, yourself," said Robin. "I am only five years old and I can't take care of a baby. I will find somebody else to take care of you."

Robin picked up the very heavy baby and walked down the street. She met a woman pushing a baby carriage. Robin said, "Excuse me, do you need a baby?"

"Heavens, no," said the woman. "I already have a baby." She went off down the street and seventeen diaper salesmen jumped out from behind a hedge and ran after her.

Robin picked up the baby
and went on down the street.
She met an old woman and
said, "Excuse me, do you
need a baby?"

"Does it pee its pants?"
said the old lady.

"Yes," said Robin.

"Yecch," said the old lady.
"Does it dirty its diaper?"

"Yes," said Robin.

"Yecch," said the old lady.
"Does it have a runny nose?"

"Yes," said Robin.

"Yecch," said the old lady.
"I already have seventeen
cats. I don't need a baby."
She went off down the street.
Seventeen cats jumped out
of a garbage can and ran
after her.

Robin picked up the baby and went down the street. She met a woman in fancy clothes. "Excuse me," said Robin, "do you need a baby?"

"Heavens, no," said the woman. "I have seventeen jobs, lots of money and no time. I don't need a baby." She went off down the street. Seventeen secretaries, nine messengers and a pizza delivery man ran after her.

"Rats," said Robin. She picked up the baby and walked down the street. She met a man. "Excuse me," she said, "do you need a baby?"

"I don't know," said the man. "Can it wash my car?"

"No," said Robin.

"Can I sell it for lots of money?"

"No," said Robin.

"Well, what is it for?" said the man.

"It is for loving and hugging and feeding and burping," said Robin.

"I certainly don't need that," said the man. He went off down the street. Nobody followed him.

Robin sat down beside the street, for the baby was getting very heavy.

"Murmel, murmel, murmel," said the baby.

"Murmel, yourself," said Robin. "What am I going to do with you?"

An enormous truck came by and stopped.

A truck driver jumped out and walked around Robin three times. Then he looked at the baby.

"Excuse me," said Robin, "do you need a baby?"

The truck driver said, "Weeeellll..."

"Murmel, murmel, murmel," said the baby.

"Did you say, 'murmel, murmel, murmel'?"asked the truck driver.

"Yes!" said the baby.

"I need you," yelled the truck driver. He picked up the baby and started walking down the street.

"Wait," said Robin, "you forgot your truck!"
"I already have seventeen trucks," said the truck driver.
"What I need is a baby..."

"YOU can have the truck."

Other books in the Munsch for Kids series: